PROFESSIONAL SPORTS LEAGUES

# MLS

BY JON MARTHALER

**CONTENT CONSULTANT**
Steven A. Bank
Paul Hastings Professor of Business Law
UCLA School of Law

**Essential Library**

An Imprint of Abdo Publishing | abdobooks.com

**ABDOBOOKS.COM**

Published by Abdo Publishing, a division of ABDO, PO Box 398166, Minneapolis, Minnesota 55439. Copyright © 2021 by Abdo Consulting Group, Inc. International copyrights reserved in all countries. No part of this book may be reproduced in any form without written permission from the publisher. Essential Library™ is a trademark and logo of Abdo Publishing.

Printed in the United States of America, North Mankato, Minnesota.
042020
092020

 THIS BOOK CONTAINS
RECYCLED MATERIALS

Cover Photos: Ringo Chiu/Zuma Wire/Alamy, foreground; Aaron M. Sprecher/AP Images, background
Interior Photos: Aaron M. Sprecher/AP Images, 4–5 (background), 14–15 (background), 26, 36 (background), 40, 50–51 (background), 58 (foreground), 61, 62, 72, 82, 88 (background), 92; Brandon Parry/Zuma Wire/Cal Sport Media/AP Images, 4–5 (foreground); Jae C. Hong/AP Images, 9, 12; Jim Mone/AP Images, 14–15 (foreground); AP Images, 20, 22; Lenny Ignelzi/AP Images, 25; John Swart/AP Images, 27; Stephen Dunn/Getty Images Sport/Getty Images, 31; D. Ross Cameron/AP Images, 34; Pablo Martinez Monsivais/AP Images, 36 (foreground); Red Line Editorial, 39, 61, 65; Anthony Souffle/Star Tribune/AP Images, 41; Michael Janosz/ISI Photos/Getty Images Sport/ Getty Images, 45; Rich von Biberstein/Icon Sportswire/AP Images, 49; Andrew Dieb/Icon Sportswire/AP Images, 50–51 (foreground); Rich Graessle/Icon Sportswire/AP Images, 54; Kevin Wolf/AP Images, 57; Kirby Lee/AP Images, 58; Mark Blinch/The Canadian Press/ AP Images, 63; Maria Lysaker/Zuma Wire/Cal Sport Media/AP Images, 69; Jon Endow/ Image of Sport/AP Images, 73; Marcio Jose Sanchez/AP Images, 75; Elaine Thompson/AP Images, 78; Andy Mead/YCJ/Icon Sportswire/AP Images, 83; Reed Saxon/AP Images, 86; Ted S. Warren/AP Images, 88 (foreground); Joseph Weiser/Icon Sportswire/AP Images, 93, 99

Editor: Arnold Ringstad
Series Designer: Dan Peluso

**LIBRARY OF CONGRESS CONTROL NUMBER: 2019954202**
**PUBLISHER'S CATALOGING-IN-PUBLICATION DATA**
Names: Marthaler, Jon, author.
Title: MLS / by Jon Marthaler
Description: Minneapolis, Minnesota : Abdo Publishing, 2021 | Series: Professional sports leagues | Includes online resources and index.
Identifiers: ISBN 9781532192074 (lib. bdg.) | ISBN 9781532179976 (ebook)
Subjects: LCSH: Major League Soccer (Organization)--Juvenile literature. | Football (Soccer)--Juvenile literature. | Professional sports franchises--Juvenile literature. | Sports--United States--History--Juvenile literature.
Classification: DDC 796.334--dc23

# CONTENTS

# CHAPTER

# EL TRÁFICO
# 2018

Superstar Zlatan Ibrahimović quickly made his mark in
MLS when he joined the league in 2018. ▶

The full-page ad on the back cover of the *Los Angeles Times* sports section read, simply, "Dear Los Angeles, You're welcome."[1] At the bottom was the signature of the Los Angeles Galaxy's newest player, striker Zlatan Ibrahimović.

The tone was entirely in keeping with the bombastic Zlatan. The Swedish superstar had played for just about every superclub in Europe—first Juventus, then Inter Milan, Barcelona, AC Milan, Paris Saint-Germain, and Manchester United. This is a man who once said, "I can't help but laugh at how perfect I am."[2] And now, in 2018, Zlatan had reached North America. He was just in time for the very first game between the Galaxy and their brand-new crosstown rivals, Los Angeles FC (LAFC).

## MAJOR LEAGUE SOCCER IN LOS ANGELES

The Los Angeles Galaxy were one of MLS's original ten teams in 1996. Like other teams from that era, their stadium is in a suburb. In this case, it's in Carson, California, which is about 15 miles (24 km) south of downtown Los Angeles. In 2005, MLS launched a second team in Los Angeles, called Chivas USA. It was so named because the owners of the team CD Guadalajara in Mexico, known as Chivas, also owned Chivas USA. Chivas USA shared the Galaxy's stadium. The new team was supposed to appeal to local fans of Latin American descent, but it was poorly managed and poorly run. In 2014, MLS shut down the team and gave its spot to Los Angeles FC, which started playing in 2018.

That Zlatan, a world superstar, would even consider coming to Major League Soccer (MLS) was a testament to how the league had grown since it first kicked off in 1996. What began as a scramble to fill out ten teams with competent players had grown to the point that it could attract one of the world's top soccer talents to Los Angeles.

## NEW TEAM, NEW RIVALRY

The Galaxy had been around since the beginning of the league, but LAFC, like Zlatan, was new to MLS. LAFC represented the second attempt to add a second team to the nation's second-largest city, one that was arguably the soccer capital of the United States. It was fitting that Zlatan's debut would be in the first crosstown rivalry game between the two clubs, taking place at the Galaxy's home stadium in the southern Los Angeles metro area.

The teams hadn't met even once, but the rivalry games already had a nickname: "El Tráfico." The name was a pun on "El Clásico," the name for matches between Barcelona and Real Madrid in Spain. The modified name was a perfect fit for crosstown games in famously traffic-choked Los Angeles. That the game had a Spanish-influenced name also made sense, given the large Hispanic population in Southern California. Before the first game was even played, fans of both teams were clashing. Murals of both teams in Los Angeles had already been defaced by rival fans.

In many ways, the game was emblematic of the history of MLS. It had a superstar European player, one who was past the age at which big-name European clubs would give him a major role. In Carlos Vela, LAFC's biggest star, it had a Latin American player who had played in Europe and then moved to the United States to dominate. It was a local rivalry with a pithy name, a game meaningful to its fans despite the teams having no history with each other. If it had been a 0–0 draw, the hype would have been wasted. Perhaps it was good that Zlatan had arrived, because a brash showman like Zlatan would never let such hype go unfulfilled.

## TIME FOR KICKOFF

It was Vela, not Zlatan, who got the fireworks started. In just the fifth minute of the match, Vela picked up a Galaxy turnover on the edge of the opposition penalty

Vela, *center*, made the first move in the 2018 edition of El Tráfico.

area. He took one touch, then blasted a curling drive into the far top corner of the net, a gorgeous goal to get the rivalry going.

Twenty minutes later, Vela was on the score sheet again. This time, he gathered a pass on the penalty spot and danced around the onrushing goalkeeper. He then doubled back slowly, almost as if he were waiting for as many defenders to scramble back as he could. By the time he softly chipped the ball, six Galaxy players were nearby, none of whom could do anything but watch as the ball floated over their heads, bounced off the crossbar, and landed gently behind the goal line. It was now 2–0 to LAFC, and the away fans celebrated as if they'd won a trophy.

Three minutes into the second half, LAFC scored what must have felt like the clinching goal. Marcos Ureña's attempted cross for Vela deflected off a Galaxy defender and into the net. Even a brand-new team would surely be able to ride a 3–0 lead to a rivalry win.

## ZLATAN ENTERS THE FRAY

But of course, there was Zlatan, who started the game on the bench because he'd just arrived two days prior to the match. The Galaxy's Sebastian Lletget was the first to cut into the deficit, splitting the LAFC defense and scoring in the 61st minute. Ten minutes later, Ibrahimović made his debut, and he immediately made an impact. An LAFC defender, ever aware of Zlatan's position, allowed the Galaxy's Emmanuel Boateng to dart in behind him and send in a crossing pass. Chris Pontius was on the

### A STAR-STUDDED OWNERS' SUITE

Most sports teams have only one owner, but in 2019 Los Angeles FC listed 31 owners on their team website. The roster included actor Will Ferrell; USA women's soccer star Mia Hamm Garciaparra and her husband, Nomar Garciaparra, who played 14 years in Major League Baseball; and basketball Hall of Famer Earvin "Magic" Johnson.

other end, powering a header into the net to make the score 3–2.

Three minutes later, MLS got its first look at the real Zlatan. A looping ball bounced over an LAFC defender's head in midfield, where Zlatan—with a full head of steam—pounced. Forty yards from the goal, with the ball descending from the high bounce, he chose to go for a low-percentage, long-range blast. Other players might have timed the volley wrong and sent the ball into the crowd, skewing wide of the net—or worse, sent it weakly dribbling to the goalkeeper. But Zlatan's drive arced neatly over the goalkeeper and slammed into the back of the net.

Now it was a tied game, and the fans were delirious. Words nearly failed Fox Sports play-by-play announcer John Strong, who could only yell, "Come on! COME ON!" in disbelief at the long-distance strike.[3] The hype was fulfilled. MLS had come a long way in 23 years, from the humble league seemingly formed overnight to a raucous game that featured Zlatan Ibrahimović scoring what would later be named Goal of the Year.

Had the game ended 3–3, it still would have been a perfect description of what MLS is all about, and it would still be remembered for Zlatan's goal. But the great man himself had one more trick up his sleeve. In stoppage time, he beat two defenders and the goalkeeper to a floating

Zlatan pulled off his shirt as he and his teammates celebrated his impressive first MLS goal.

cross and directed his header just inside the far post, nestling the game winner into the side netting.

## GALAXY 4, LAFC 3

MLS has seen plenty of star players come and go. These players have come from North America, Latin America, and around the world. The league has seen teams rise and fall.

It's seen rivalries develop all over the continent, and it's seen its teams compete against the best teams that the rest of North and South America have to offer. But Galaxy 4, LAFC 3, with two goals from Carlos Vela and two more from Zlatan Ibrahimović, might be the best of what MLS's first quarter century offered to soccer fans in Canada and the United States.

It wasn't the first soccer league in the United States and Canada, nor the only one to capture the attention of North American sports fans. The ones that came before, though, all eventually failed. What makes MLS different, more than anything else, is not its struggles but its survival.

## SOCCER AT THE 1984 SUMMER OLYMPICS

The tournament that proved that fans in the United States would come out for soccer games was the soccer tournament at the 1984 Summer Olympics. One of the semifinals, the bronze medal match, and the gold medal match were all held at the Rose Bowl in Los Angeles. Attendance for all three matches topped 95,000. The gold medal match between France and Brazil saw 101,799 people in the stands.[4] The game set an American soccer attendance record that wouldn't be topped for 30 years.

# CHAPTER 2

# AMERICAN PROFESSIONAL SOCCER

Not until the NASL formed in the late 1960s would professional soccer find any measure of widespread success in the United States. ▶

14

Since 1996, MLS has been the top level of men's professional soccer in the United States and Canada. The history of pro soccer on the continent goes back much further than 1996, though, stretching back to the early days of pro sports in the United States.

Local leagues were organized across the country in the 1890s and early 1900s, mostly among immigrants to America who were already familiar with soccer. The United States Football Association (USFA), which is now called the US Soccer Federation (USSF), was founded in 1913. The organization is still in charge of sanctioning pro and amateur soccer in the United States. It organized the National Challenge Cup. This was the first nationwide opportunity for newly formed soccer clubs to compete. The tournament is still going today, though it is now called the US Open Cup.

## THE AMERICAN SOCCER LEAGUE

The first professional league to expand beyond a small area was the American Soccer League (ASL), which was founded in 1921. It was based in the northeastern United States, one of the two strongholds of soccer in America after World War I (1914–1918). The other stronghold was Saint Louis, Missouri. Teams from Massachusetts, Rhode Island, New Jersey, New York, and Pennsylvania made up the eight-team ASL. It relied mostly on immigrant players who worked for clubs based at industrial companies, such as Bethlehem Steel in Pennsylvania.

The American sports world was very different then. Baseball, college football, and boxing were extremely popular, but none of the other major pro sports of today were well established. Sensing an opportunity to make money, baseball team owners and other businessmen started buying soccer teams. A man named Sam Mark bought the Fall River, Massachusetts, team and renamed it the Marksmen after himself. He built a 15,000-seat stadium for the team. This made him perhaps the first American to see a soccer stadium as a moneymaking opportunity.

The league enjoyed a brief spell of popularity. Within ten years, though, disagreements with the USFA and the onset of the Great Depression, a severe worldwide economic downturn, hurt the league severely. By the 1930s, fan interest was low, and the money was gone—a story that

## ARCHIE STARK, GOAL MACHINE

Born in Glasgow, Scotland, but raised in New Jersey, Archie Stark became the greatest goal scorer the ASL had ever seen. After joining Bethlehem Steel in 1924, Stark scored 67 goals in 44 matches. Ed Sullivan, a sportswriter who later became the host of TV's *Ed Sullivan Show*, dubbed him the "Babe Ruth of soccer."[1] Stark scored 54 goals the next season as well. He still holds the record for most goals in a first division season, as well as the most goals in a first division career (260).

would become familiar to American soccer fans. It was clear that soccer was not going to be America's winter pastime, as much as the ASL had tried to make it so. Other pro sports grew to fill the void. Once again, the local leagues became the home of American soccer. Until the 1960s, soccer was reduced to a mostly regional, mostly amateur game in the United States.

# THE NORTH AMERICAN SOCCER LEAGUE

By the 1960s, all of the ingredients were in place for the United States to give a national league another try.

## THE INTERNATIONAL SOCCER LEAGUE

In 1960, Bill Cox revived soccer in the United States with an ingenious idea. Cox had noticed that summer tours of the United States by big name European teams tended to draw lots of fans, especially fans from the teams' home countries. His idea for a league was to simply borrow those teams for a summer league season, and so the International Soccer League was born. Between 1960 and 1965, famous European teams such as Bayern Munich, Everton, West Ham United, Red Star Belgrade, and Sporting Lisbon played five- or six-game league seasons in the United States in the summer.

Most of the games were played in New York, but some were played in other cities as well. It wasn't exactly an American soccer league, but it brought big-time soccer to the United States all the same. Clive Toye, who later brought Pelé to America, summed it up: "Without Bill Cox, there wouldn't have been anything. If you want to simplify it, no Bill Cox, no me, no Phil Woosnam, no NASL, no Pelé. Nothing."[2]

Nationwide jet travel had shortened the travel time between cities, and television was beaming sports into US households. This included, for the first time, soccer from around the world. In 1966, millions of Americans watched the World Cup final on NBC. These factors convinced enough potential team owners that soccer could succeed in the United States and that television would pay for it.

The result was the North American Soccer League (NASL), which from the very beginning was determined to offer a different style of soccer from that traditionally found around the world. At the time, European soccer wasn't known for being the fast-paced game found in today's Champions League and Premier League. Violence in the crowd was common at matches. A typical match in England might be a dull 1–1 draw played out on a muddy field in freezing weather. Said Rodney Marsh, one of the stars of the NASL and a native Englishman, "English football is a gray game played on a gray day before gray people. American soccer is a colorful game played on a sunny day before colorful people."[3]

## BRIGHT, SHINY, NEW SOCCER

The NASL was determined to make soccer an entertainment event, like the National Football League (NFL), rather than a mud-spattered tug-of-war. Out went traditional soccer. In came brightly colored uniforms with names and numbers

NASL player Rodney Marsh rode out onto the field on a motorcycle before a 1976 game.

on the back, making the sport more accessible for TV viewers. In came rules designed to promote scoring, with bonus points in the standings for making extra goals. To keep games from finishing in draws, in came a penalty shoot-out to end tied matches. Even the shoot-out itself was different. Instead of merely taking a kick from the penalty spot, players were given the ball 35 yards from goal and had five seconds to take a shot at the solo goalkeeper.

## A LEAGUE WITH RECYCLED TEAMS

Before the NASL could get off the ground in 1968, a rival league, the National Professional Soccer League (NPSL), began playing in 1967. The NASL owners decided that they needed to start their own league in 1967 as well, one year ahead of their plan. They renamed themselves the United Soccer Association (USA) and simply imported entire professional teams from around the world. They also took the confusing step of renaming the teams. Ireland's Shamrock Rovers became the Boston Rovers. Cagliari of Italy became the Chicago Mustangs. The Wolverhampton Wanderers from England, the eventual league champions, became the Los Angeles Wolves. Crowds were small, and the USA and the NPSL merged for the 1968 season.

After launching in 1968, the NASL struggled. Twelve of the league's 17 teams folded after the first season. In 1969, the league imported entire foreign teams to play the first half of the season and gave the teams the names and jerseys of NASL teams. For example, the English team Aston Villa played as the Atlanta Chiefs. In the second half of the season, the NASL replaced the foreign players with local ones. Throughout the entire span of the NASL, teams came and went regularly. Between 1968 and 1984, 41 cities in the United States and Canada hosted an NASL team.[4] None of those cities hosted a team for the entire span of the league. Chaos was the name of the game, at least in terms of remembering which team was in which city.

Pelé (10) brought his skills and stardom to the NASL in 1975.

## PELÉ AND THE COSMOS

The league's flagship franchise was the New York Cosmos, founded in 1971 and owned by a record company. Like all NASL teams, the Cosmos struggled for a few years to draw fans. But in a prestigious city like New York, struggling for relevance wasn't good enough. And what better way to get relevant, team owners thought, than to sign the one soccer player that the entire world, even Americans, had heard of: Pelé.

By the time he came to America, Pelé was already a Brazilian legend, and known as the world's greatest-ever soccer player. He was the youngest person ever to win the World Cup in 1958, and lifted the trophy in 1962 and 1970 as well. He is still the only player to win it three times. He'd already scored more than 1,000 goals for Santos, his club in Brazil. FIFA, the international governing body of soccer, named him Player of the Century in 2000.

Pelé was already retired. He also wasn't easy to get out of Brazil. The government was so disinclined to let him go that it had passed a law declaring him a national treasure and had to approve him even leaving the country. None of that stopped the Cosmos, who even got US secretary of state Henry Kissinger to call Pelé to convince him that his future was in America. And so in June 1975, Pelé signed on the dotted line and agreed to become the centerpiece of the Cosmos.

Pelé wasn't the only famous player to come to America. New York also signed German star Franz Beckenbauer and flashy Italian playmaker Giorgio Chinaglia. Los Angeles signed Northern Irish legend George Best. Boston, then Toronto, had Portuguese legend Eusebio. It worked, for a while. New York drew huge crowds throughout the Pelé era and into the early 1980s. Teams in Minnesota, Tampa Bay, and Seattle regularly attracted more than 25,000 fans to games. But other franchises struggled. For example, in 1978, the Cosmos averaged almost 50,000 fans a game, while ten of the league's other 23 teams failed to get an average of even 10,000.[5]

## THE END OF THE NASL

Even with all those fans and all those stars, nobody involved with the league was making much money. In 1980, none of the league's teams were profitable, and combined, the 24 teams lost more than $30 million.[6] When an economic recession hit the United States, fans didn't have much money to attend games, and owners didn't have the resources to tempt foreign players. The league had never developed American players, so it couldn't fall back on local talent.

The end finally came when the New York Cosmos could no longer afford to play. The company that owned the Cosmos, Warner Communications, was losing money on other things besides soccer, and so it had to sell the team. Without Warner's money, the Cosmos couldn't pay big money to all their players. When New York folded before the 1985 season, so did six more of the league's remaining nine

The MISL kept American pro soccer alive in the 1980s, but a new outdoor league, MLS, was on the horizon.

teams. A league with just two teams would be impossible. It was the final whistle for the NASL.

The end of the NASL didn't mean pro soccer was dead in America. There was still an indoor soccer league, the Major Indoor Soccer League (MISL), which played on artificial turf in hockey rinks. But the nation's first attempt at a nationwide, outdoor, top-rate pro soccer league was ending in failure. It would take another decade—and the arrival of soccer's biggest tournament—to give the United States another shot at a league, one that would try very hard to learn the lessons of the NASL's failure.

# CHAPTER 3

# NEW LEAGUE, NEW RULES, NEW TEAMS

Excitement around the 1994 World Cup, held in the United States, set the stage for the revival of American professional soccer in the years to come. ▶

**M**LS kicked off in 1996, but in a sense the league was really born years earlier, on July 4, 1988. On that day, FIFA announced that the United States would host the World Cup in 1994. Soccer's biggest tournament would take place on American soil for the first time. While plenty of people insisted that fans in the United States would ignore the tournament, FIFA was confident that it could make money in America. And while it was at it, the organization required the United States to get another professional soccer league off the ground.

## THE WORLD CUP THAT COULD HAVE SAVED AMERICAN SOCCER

The 1994 World Cup helped MLS get going. But had the World Cup come to America earlier, the NASL might never have folded. In 1986, Colombia was supposed to host the World Cup. However, the country had to back out. The two main candidates for a replacement were Mexico, which had hosted the tournament just 16 years before, and the United States.

The NASL did its best to push for the tournament, but the US Soccer Federation (USSF) did not. A *Sports Illustrated* article even accused a USSF officer of calling FIFA president João Havelange to inform him that the United States was "not ready" to host the tournament. USSF president Gene Edwards was quoted as saying, "We would have really messed it up."[1] FIFA awarded the tournament to Mexico. Had it chosen to move the tournament to the United States instead, the NASL might have survived due to increased interest in soccer in the United States, just as MLS was driven by the success of the tournament in 1994.

# THE 1994 WORLD CUP

The 1994 World Cup was a hit, setting an attendance record that still stood as of the 2018 World Cup. Even more importantly, the United States did well. The US men's national soccer team hadn't won a World Cup game since 1950. It hadn't even qualified for the tournament between 1950 and 1990. The 1994 World Cup was its coming-out party. The United States earned a 1–1 draw with Switzerland and then beat South American powerhouse Colombia 2–1. They were the first points the team had earned at the World Cup in nearly a half century. The team qualified for the knockout rounds before losing 1–0 to Brazil.

For the first time, American fans had American players to cheer for. Striker Eric Wynalda scored with a booming free kick against Switzerland. Defender Alexi Lalas became an immediate icon for both his shaggy red hair and goatee and his physical defending. Midfielders John Harkes and Tab Ramos, goalkeeper Tony Meola, and defender Marcelo Balboa—best known for attempting a bicycle kick against Colombia—were, if not household names, at least popular enough to become the first generation of American soccer stars.

# ANYTHING BUT NASL 2.0

MLS launched in 1996 with a key goal in mind: don't repeat the mistakes of the NASL. Rather than have teams constantly moving and folding, in MLS all of the teams would be owned by the league. Rather than have a team like the Cosmos that could consistently outspend the other teams, MLS would have a salary budget for each team. It would be set relatively low, around $1.1 million.[2] No team could spend itself into bankruptcy, because the league controlled the teams. The aim was stability rather than chaos.

The league kicked off in 1996 with ten teams. Unfortunately, some of those teams had regrettable names, and all of them had regrettable jerseys. The new league let companies such as Nike, Reebok, and Adidas name the teams and design the jerseys, and the companies got carried away with trying to make them seem new and different. D.C. United had a traditional soccer name, but the rest of the teams had names many fans found confusing, like the San Jose Clash, the Dallas Burn, and the Kansas City Wiz.

## MARCELO BALBOA'S BICYCLE KICK

Defender Marcelo Balboa didn't score in the 1994 World Cup, yet he still became well known for his acrobatic attempt to score from a corner kick against Colombia. With his back to goal, Balboa launched his lower body high into the air to attempt to kick the ball backward over his own head, a soccer move known as a bicycle kick. Balboa missed, but the move made such an impression on fans that owner Phil Anschutz only agreed to invest in MLS if he could have Balboa on his team.

Eric Wynalda sent the first goal in MLS history into the back of the net.

The league launched with the best-known players from the 1994 US World Cup team, a few South Americans, Italian standout Roberto Donadoni, and a huge number of lesser-known players. But it was a true top-division professional league, and soccer was back in the United States. Wynalda scored the league's first goal, with his San Jose Clash beating D.C. United 1–0 in the inaugural game on April 6, 1996.

## FAMILIAR STRUGGLES

In the first season, the teams in the biggest markets—the New York/New Jersey MetroStars and the Los Angeles Galaxy—led the league in attendance, drawing more than 20,000 fans a game.[3] At the start of the 1997 season, the league announced it would add its first two expansion teams in 1998, in Chicago and Miami. However, that early momentum wouldn't last long.

MLS hadn't been confident enough to abandon every bit of the NASL legacy. For example, to prevent matches from ending in ties, the league still used the NASL-style penalty shoot-out. It also experimented with other rule changes. This included allowing four substitutes instead of three, with the fourth being reserved only for the goalkeeper. It also had the game time displayed on a scoreboard rather than kept on the field by the referee.

Soccer purists hated these changes, and the new rules weren't drawing new fans to the league. Attendance was down. Television viewership was minuscule. The league

## THREE LEAGUES

In 1993, three leagues were competing to earn US Soccer's sanction as the country's first division league. MLS eventually won that vote. It helped that league organizer Alan Rothenberg was also the US Soccer Federation president. There had been two other candidates. One was the five-team American Professional Soccer League, which was already playing games. The other was a strange proposal by a businessman named Jim Paglia. It was called League 1 America. Paglia's plan involved an entirely new version of soccer, in which certain players could not go into certain areas of the field. There would be multiple goals at each end of the field, and goals would be worth different values depending on who scored them and from where. This plan got little backing.

never could find a local investor to run the Tampa Bay Mutiny, and the Miami Fusion were struggling to attract fans. After the 2001 season, MLS decided that both Florida franchises would cease operations. This left the league with ten teams.

## THE 2002 WORLD CUP AND TENTATIVE EXPANSION

Once again, the World Cup helped save the league. In the summer of 2002, the US national team made a surprising run to the quarterfinals of the World Cup. This included wins against heavily favored Portugal and longtime rival Mexico along the way. In many ways, it was another 1994, and a new generation of American players, such as Landon Donovan and DaMarcus Beasley, was suddenly the hope of the future.

The chief investors in MLS, Phil Anschutz and Lamar Hunt, owned or partly owned all but one of the league's teams. The two had partnered with the league to buy the TV rights to the 2002 and 2006 World Cup. They then turned around and resold those rights to American TV companies along with the MLS rights. This guaranteed that MLS would stay on TV. That investment paid off with the 2002 World Cup team's success.

MLS also transitioned from removing teams to again adding new ones, especially teams that could promise to

Donovan became one of America's biggest soccer stars following the 2002 World Cup.

build soccer-specific stadiums. The first to be announced was Salt Lake City in 2004. This was a surprise since Salt Lake City was not the kind of big city that the league had previously targeted. But the owners had a plan to build a new stadium, and they wouldn't need to be bailed out by Anschutz and Hunt. That was all MLS needed to award a franchise. The league also announced a novel experiment in Los Angeles, adding a second team in the soccer-mad region, which would be run by the owners of Mexican giant Chivas Guadalajara and called Chivas USA. Multiple other cities had expressed some interest in starting a team as well, just a few years after MLS had to fold two franchises. Things were looking up, and the league hoped to capitalize by bringing in the biggest name it knew.

## THE BECKHAM EXPERIMENT

In 1975, when Pelé signed to play in the NASL, he was soccer's most famous player. If people knew who any soccer player was, it was virtually certain they knew about Pelé. In 2006, the equivalent player was David Beckham, the Real Madrid midfielder who'd become a global celebrity. Luckily for MLS, Beckham also harbored a fondness for the United States. In 2007, the Los Angeles Galaxy made a deal to sign Beckham to the league's biggest contract. His debut was set to come after Real Madrid's season was complete. He'd earn plenty of money. But his goals in coming to the United States were nothing short of changing how people thought about American soccer. "If I can make a difference and make people more aware and make kids realize that you can actually go into higher levels and make a great living playing soccer, that's what I'm going over there to do," he said.[4]

He certainly brought plenty of attention with him. His introductory news conference in July 2007 brought 5,000 fans, 700 media members, 65 TV cameras, and a news helicopter to the Galaxy's stadium.[5] By the time he debuted,

# DAVID
# BECKHAM

When David Beckham came to Major League Soccer in 2007, he may not have been the world's best soccer player, but he was definitely the best-known player in the world. He had become a famous athlete playing for Manchester United and the England national team. He had become a celebrity after he married Victoria Beckham, who was part of the 1990s pop group the Spice Girls.

Throughout his soccer career, people tried to dismiss him as a celebrity rather than a serious player, but wherever he went, he ended up winning fans over with hard work. The same thing happened with the Los Angeles Galaxy, where his first two years with the team were a struggle. After his second year, he played half a year with AC Milan in Italy, leading to a confrontation with Galaxy fans who were holding signs that said "Go home fraud" and "Part-time player."[6] But Beckham kept working, and though he missed much of 2010 with an injury, he helped the Galaxy win the MLS Cup in 2011 and 2012.

◄ Beckham's arrival in MLS helped boost the league's profile and popularity.

ESPN had been running promos for two weeks hyping his arrival. It was the sort of attention that MLS had long craved.

In terms of hype, Beckham's arrival was a wild success. In soccer terms, it was a bit more uneven. The Galaxy missed the playoffs both of the first two seasons Beckham was there. However, the longer he stayed, the better the team got. The Galaxy reached the MLS Cup finals in 2009, 2011, and 2012, winning the latter two in Beckham's final two seasons in Los Angeles.

## TORONTO, SEATTLE, AND MLS 2.0

Before Toronto FC joined the league in 2007 and the Seattle Sounders joined in 2009, MLS looked very different than it does today. Teams either played in mostly empty NFL stadiums or built new fields in far-flung suburbs. The idea was to draw suburban families with soccer-playing kids who would get interested in MLS because they played the sport.

Toronto changed all of that by building a stadium downtown rather than off in the suburbs. They catered to young urban fans rather than suburban families. Seattle followed two years later, marketing itself to the same kind of dedicated die-hard fans. Seattle even gave its fans a chance to vote out the general manager every four years, its own version of European clubs electing a club president. The Sounders immediately began leading the league in attendance in their own downtown stadium, which was shared with the NFL's Seahawks.

The success of Toronto and Seattle changed MLS. It gave a blueprint for future expansion clubs to follow. MLS was no longer just about families heading out to the suburbs in their minivans to catch a game. Now, the league catered to dedicated fans, those who marched and cheered and sang and waved flags.

In 2006, the San Jose franchise moved to Houston, and San Jose had to wait until 2008 to get a new franchise. In 2014, the league shut down Chivas USA, and the franchise was reborn as Los Angeles FC in 2018. Other than those two hiccups, the league has been in growth mode ever since the 2002 World Cup. The league is set to include 30 teams in 2022. That includes a new team in Miami partly owned by David Beckham.

The goal of MLS all along was to survive, to get American soccer fans interested, and to keep them interested. The NASL got people watching soccer briefly, but when the big names left and the money dried up, the league itself withered away. With the growth MLS has enjoyed over the years, it looks like it's here to stay.

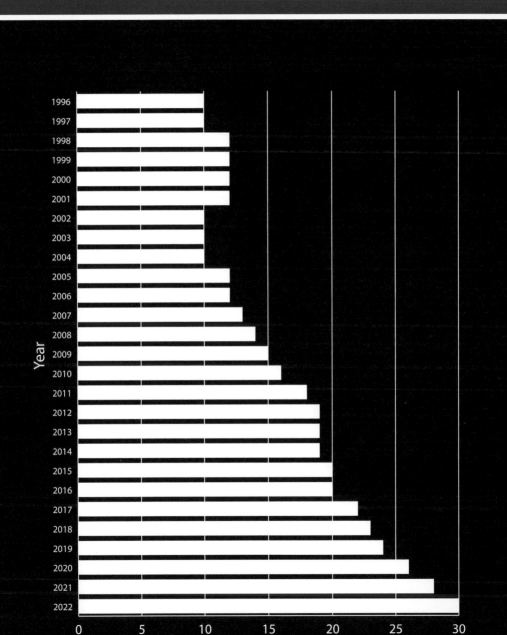

# CHAPTER 4

# CATHEDRALS OF AMERICAN SOCCER

Fans can find an exciting atmosphere at MLS's newest stadiums, such as Minnesota United's Allianz Field, which ▶ opened in 2019.

**A** tour through the stadiums used by MLS teams is a tour through the history of the league itself. At various points during the league's existence, there have been four distinct ideas about the best places for MLS teams to play. All four types of these stadiums still exist in the league today.

## NFL AND THE BIRTH OF MLS

The first type is the NFL stadium, in which the MLS team is a secondary tenant—or worse. This setup is a relic of the early days of the league. When MLS launched in 1996, the teams were brand new. None of them had their own stadium to call home. Every team had to find a stadium to play in, and those stadiums were usually the local NFL venues. Kansas City played at Arrowhead Stadium, home of the NFL's Chiefs. Colorado played at Mile High Stadium, home of the Broncos. The New York/New Jersey MetroStars played at Giants Stadium. Coincidentally, this was the same place the NASL's New York Cosmos had played.

Even if teams drew 15,000 fans or more for soccer games, the atmosphere in those stadiums was completely lost in a sea of empty seats. NFL stadiums often have 60,000 seats or more. Plus, since the fields were football fields, most of them had football markings on them. The soccer field markings were hard to see on top of the hash marks, yard lines, and numbers on an NFL field.

## CONVERSION PAINS

MLS's first game ever was held on April 6, 1996, at Spartan Stadium in San Jose, California. The stadium is usually used for San Jose State University football games, and not everything was quite ready for soccer. The shiny silver poles that held the lights illuminating the field for night games created a glare for the cameras and had to be painted the day before the game. The San Jose Clash's general manager also had the stadium crew paint the MLS logo at midfield, which is common in American football but against the rules of soccer. MLS executives made them paint green over the logo.

The best remaining example of this stadium setup is the New England Revolution. The Revs play in Gillette Stadium, the home of the NFL's New England Patriots. The Revolution had an average attendance of more than 16,000 in 2019, but Gillette Stadium has a capacity of 65,878.[1] This meant that the Revolution averaged playing in front of almost 50,000 empty seats at every home match.

# SOCCER-SPECIFIC STADIUMS

MLS knew that if the league was going to survive, it needed its own soccer stadiums. "I'm not sure we adequately gauged the difficulty of playing in overly large American football stadiums," said MLS owner Lamar Hunt.[2] The Columbus Crew, Hunt's team, were the first MLS team to find their own place to play. They built a stadium with just over 22,000 seats on the grounds of the Ohio State Fair in

Columbus. This replaced games at Ohio Stadium, Ohio State University's football stadium, which seats more than 100,000 people. The change worked for the Crew, which led the league in attendance in 1999, the year the stadium opened. Fans really seemed to enjoy the soccer-specific setup.

The second team to move into its own home was the Los Angeles Galaxy. They built a 27,000-seat stadium in Carson, California, south of Los Angeles. Located on the campus of California State University–Dominguez Hills, the complex also included a tennis stadium, a track-and-field stadium, and a cycling velodrome. In many ways, what was then called the Home Depot Center (it became Dignity

## CREW STADIUM, THE HOME OF "DOS A CERO"

When the United States men's national team plays Mexico, the stadium is usually full of Mexican fans, even if the game is held in the United States. In 2001, with a key qualifier for the 2002 World Cup coming up, US Soccer set out to change that. It wanted to give the United States a home field advantage. The natural location was MLS's only soccer-specific stadium, in Columbus. The fact that the game was played in the dead of winter made it even better.

It was so cold that Mexico waited in its heated dressing room before the game, skipping the usual warm-up on the field. Not surprisingly, Mexico was a step slow that day, and the United States won 2–0. It was the beginning of a trend. In 2005, 2009, and 2013, the United States returned to Columbus to host Mexico in the World Cup qualifiers. Each time, the US team won 2–0, or "Dos a cero," as the US fans chanted at their Spanish-speaking Mexican counterparts. The streak was only broken in 2016, when Mexico won 2–1 in Columbus.

Dignity Health Sports Park in California is the largest soccer-specific stadium in the United States.

Health Sports Park in 2019) was the crown jewel of this era of MLS stadiums.

The Home Depot Center was a perfect example of the second era of MLS stadiums. It was built in a suburb and surrounded by other activities. This is the model that Dallas, Chicago, Colorado, and Salt Lake copied in the following years. All of them built stadiums in far-flung suburban locations.

# GOING DOWNTOWN

Toronto FC joined MLS in 2007. The team played in a brand-new stadium called BMO Field, built not out in the suburbs but downtown, on the site of Exhibition Stadium. This was where baseball's Toronto Blue Jays and the Canadian Football League's Toronto Argonauts had once played. The new team took until its fifth home game to score a goal at home. But when it happened, the fans were ready to mark the occasion.

Twenty-three minutes into the game, Toronto forward Edson Buddle pounced on a loose ball in the Chicago penalty area. He rolled in a cross toward the middle of the field. Toronto forward Danny Dichio was the first to reach the ball. He poked it into the corner of the goal and touched off a celebration the league had never seen. When the team had handed out seat cushions as promotional items that day, they may not have understood just how far seat cushions might fly if thrown like Frisbees. Thousands of fans enthusiastically tossed their cushions, and they rained down on the field.

Building a stadium downtown, rather than out in the suburbs, was bound to attract a different type of fan. Instead of moms and dads and kids, young, urban fans were coming to games. These new fans were passionate and rowdy enough to toss their seat cushions after a goal was scored. The atmosphere in Toronto was electric. It wasn't just about how many tickets had been sold but about how loud the stadiums were and how committed the fans were.

The league took notice, and since Toronto, most teams have built stadiums in urban areas as near to the city center as they can manage. Teams in Los Angeles, Portland, Houston, Minnesota, and Orlando have all put their stadiums in their city's urban core. They're catering to a new set of fans who are younger, louder, and perhaps even more likely to toss a promotional item.

## FILLING NFL STADIUMS

As the league has grown, several teams have tested out a new idea that goes back to the dawn of the league. What if they played in an NFL stadium and filled the whole thing? The first team to try it was Seattle, who moved into CenturyLink Field

## PROVIDENCE PARK

The Portland Timbers play at Providence Park in downtown Portland, Oregon. Its history long predates MLS's history. It was built in 1926, and it has hosted minor-league baseball, college football, and even dog racing. Today, though it's been remodeled to be entirely for soccer, vestiges of its past are still visible for visitors. These include a curved stand that used to surround the baseball infield, as well as the balcony on the Multnomah Athletic Club where club members can still watch games at the stadium the club built nearly 100 years ago. Its atmosphere and its history are second to none. This is why in 2017, soccer magazine *FourFourTwo* named it the best soccer stadium in America.

alongside the Seattle Seahawks in 2009, the Sounders' first year in MLS. The stadium, at the southern end of downtown, was close enough for fans to gather downtown and then march to matches. This gave game day a distinctly urban feeling. The Sounders immediately shot to the top of the MLS attendance charts. In 2019, they had the twenty-ninth best attendance of any soccer team in the world, averaging 42,797 fans per match.[3] This was more than for famous international teams like Chelsea, Juventus, or AC Milan.

Atlanta United, which entered the league in 2017, did even better. Like the Sounders, Atlanta plays in a brand-new local NFL stadium. Atlanta's success and the spacious new stadium meant that the Five Stripes, as the Atlanta team is nicknamed, averaged 51,457 fans in 2017 and 2018.[4] This was the tenth-best attendance of any soccer team in the world.

## ROLE REVERSAL

The early days of MLS saw teams playing in mostly empty NFL stadiums. In 2017, the tables were turned, as the NFL's San Diego Chargers moved to Los Angeles. They had to rent their stadium from the Los Angeles Galaxy. The Chargers struggled to draw fans in Los Angeles, making many NFL people wonder whether they could survive there. In two decades, people have gone from wondering whether MLS teams can survive in NFL stadiums to wondering whether an NFL team can survive in an MLS stadium.

Atlanta United attracts huge, passionate crowds to their games at Mercedes-Benz Stadium.

New teams coming into the league will follow the trend and seek to build new urban stadiums like the one in Toronto. Even teams that once built suburban stadiums have recognized the success of this new model. Chicago has played in Bridgeview, Illinois, since 2006. But starting in 2020, the Fire will move out of their suburban, soccer-specific home. Instead, they are returning to Soldier Field, the home of the NFL's Bears, where the Fire played in 1998 when the team first entered MLS.

# CHAPTER 5

# GREATS OF THE GAME

The legendary Landon Donovan played his last MLS game in 2016. ▸

Any discussion of the greatest MLS players of all time starts with Landon Donovan. Perhaps the single best piece of evidence for his greatness and influence is that the league's most valuable player (MVP) trophy is named for him. And his numbers are staggering. Donovan, who played four years for the San Jose Earthquakes and 11 for the Los Angeles Galaxy, retired as the league's all-time leader in both goals (145) and assists (136). He's since been passed on the goal-scoring list. He made the MLS All-Star Team 14 consecutive seasons, from 2001 through 2014. Curiously, he only won the MVP award once, in 2008, but he was named to the league's Best XI seven times. He also retired with plenty of championship rings. He won six MLS Cups, two MLS Supporters' Shields, and a US Open Cup.

## THE LEAGUE AWARDS

At the end of each season, MLS gives out a number of individual awards. The most coveted is the Landon Donovan MVP award. The league also has special awards for Defender of the Year, Goalkeeper of the Year, and Coach of the Year.

Many leagues have a Rookie of the Year award, and MLS does too, but it also gives out a Newcomer of the Year award. The distinction between the two is that the Rookie of the Year award goes to a player who has had no professional experience before joining the league while Newcomer of the Year goes to a player with previous professional experience who's in his first year in MLS, such as Zlatan in 2018. MLS also gives awards for Goal of the Year and Save of the Year.

Many of MLS's greatest players have been European veterans who've made names for themselves overseas and then brought their talents to the states. Donovan is still a rare gem in that he was an American-born superstar who chose to play in America. As of 2019, he also leads the US men's national team in virtually every category. This includes goals (57, tied with Clint Dempsey), and assists (58). Quite simply, he's the best American player ever.

## EUROPEAN STARS MAKING THEIR MARK

While David Beckham is the best-known of the European soccer stars who have made a career in MLS, he's by no means the only one. And no European player scored more goals in MLS than another Englishman: Bradley Wright-Phillips. The son of former Crystal Palace and Arsenal great Ian Wright, Wright-Phillips didn't make his MLS debut until the age of 28, after playing for several English teams. After coming to the New York Red Bulls, he immediately started pouring in goals. In 2018, Wright-Phillips became the fastest MLS player to score 100 career goals, and he was the first-ever two-time winner of the league's Golden Boot Award, given to the league's top scorer.[1]

With New York, Wright-Phillips followed in the footsteps of another European striker with Arsenal connections, French great Thierry Henry. In four and a half seasons

Wright-Phillips played seven seasons with the New York Red Bulls.

with New York between 2010 and 2013, Henry scored 51 goals and was named to the league's Best XI three times. Robbie Keane shot to fame playing for Arsenal's North London rivals, Tottenham Hotspur. He came to MLS in 2011 and immediately had a similar impact. Over parts of six seasons, Keane scored 83 times, winning the league MVP award in 2014 and being part of the league's Best XI on four occasions.

Of course, if you ask Zlatan Ibrahimović, he'll tell you exactly who the best player in MLS history is: Zlatan. "I've done good things, amazing things, and perfect things," he said. "I think I'm the best-ever player in MLS."[2] With 52 goals in 56 games, it's hard to argue with him. He's certainly among the best goal scorers in league history and certainly one of the best European imports.

## THE LATIN AMERICAN INFLUENCE

MLS has also seen plenty of stars come from across Latin America. One of the league's earliest stars was midfielder Carlos Valderrama, who'd long been a star in his native Colombia. He captained the Colombian national team in three World Cups, including the 1994 World Cup in the United States. He became well known in that tournament partially for his play and partially for his distinctive shock of bushy orange hair. Valderrama came to MLS in 1996 and quickly became a star, winning the league MVP award in his first season. In 2019, he was fourth on the all-time MLS list, with 114 assists.

### DESIGNATED PLAYERS

MLS has a salary budget, since the league pays the players. As of 2019, the budget is $4.24 million.[3] There are exceptions to that rule, the most important of which is the Designated Player rule. Only the first $530,000 of a Designated Player's salary counts against the salary budget. Anything beyond that amount is the responsibility of the team, not the league's central office. Each team can have up to three Designated Players.

Jaime Moreno and Marco Etcheverry also played in the 1994 World Cup, for Bolivia. Both joined D.C. United in the 1996 season. As teammates, they became the driving force behind D.C. United's early dominance of the league. Etcheverry won the league's MVP award in 1998, a season in which both Etcheverry and Moreno hit double figures in both goals and assists. The pair was a key reason that D.C. took home three of the first four MLS Cups. Etcheverry left MLS in 2003, after racking up 101 assists in eight seasons, while Moreno played on until 2010, retiring with 133 goals and 102 assists. He was the only player other than Donovan to break the 100 mark in both categories as of 2019.

Carlos Vela joined Los Angeles FC for its inaugural season in 2018 and quickly became a star. In 2019, he smashed the league record for goals in a season, tallying 34 goals in 31 games. Vela, who is also a star for Mexico's national team, was named the league's MVP for his record-setting 2019 season. Another Mexican superstar, Javier "Chicharito" Hernandez, signed with the LA Galaxy in 2020.

# THE HOMEGROWN PLAYERS

Of course, it's not just European and Latin American players who have dominated in MLS. Plenty of great players have come from the United States or made their names in the country. By the time MLS kicked off in 1996, Predrag

D.C. United recognized Moreno, *left*, as a member of its Hall of Tradition in 2013.

Radosavljević—known simply as Preki—was already nearing 33 years old. Born in Yugoslavia, he'd come to the United States in 1985 and become an indoor-soccer star, as well as an American citizen. In a ten-year career spent almost entirely with Kansas City, he became an outdoor star as well. Preki is still the only person to win the league MVP award twice, taking the trophy in 1997 and 2003. He was the league's top scorer in both seasons, with the second season coming when he had reached the age of 40. After retiring in 2005, he became a coach with Chivas USA, winning the league's Coach of the Year award in 2007.

# LANDON
# DONOVAN

Landon Donovan is known for his success with the US national team, the San Jose Earthquakes, and the Los Angeles Galaxy. But for a long time, Donovan was known partly for being the American soccer star who could take over the world and yet didn't want to go.

At the age of 17, Donovan signed with German club Bayer Leverkusen. He didn't adapt well to German culture and was homesick for Southern California. He spent much of his time playing with the US U-17 team and never played for Leverkusen's first team. In 2001, Leverkusen loaned him to San Jose.

After four successful years with San Jose, Leverkusen ended the loan and tried to bring him back to Germany. But again Donovan was homesick. He stayed only two and a half months before moving permanently back to MLS. Most agree that he is the best field player the United States ever produced. But they can't help wondering what might have been if he'd stayed in Germany and tried to make his name there.

Donovan remained active in pro soccer after retiring, helping found a second division team in San Diego, California, in 2019.

MLS has had many good defenders, but none were great for longer than Chad Marshall. He played 16 seasons for the Columbus Crew and Seattle Sounders. Over that span, Marshall played 409 games, the fourth-most in league history as of 2019. He collected three MLS Defender of the Year awards, the only man to do so. He was also named to the league Best XI four times, with the first and the last coming ten years apart.

Chris Wondolowski was such an afterthought when he came into the league in 2005 that he didn't even get picked in the MLS SuperDraft. He had to wait for the Supplemental Draft, which came afterward. Even then, he had to wait until the fourth round. He had to fight for playing time for years, and after six seasons, he had just seven goals to his name.

All of that makes it even more amazing that in 2010 he burst onto the scene with 18 goals for San Jose. He hasn't stopped scoring since. The player nicknamed "Wondo" won the Golden Boot that season and then again in 2012 when he tied the league record with 27 goals and won the league MVP award. He's scored double-digit goals every season since his breakout, and he has become the league's all-time leading scorer with 159 goals.

# THE GOALKEEPERS

The one place that the United States has always seemed to be able to keep up with the rest of the world is in the net, and MLS has seen many outstanding goalkeepers. Tim Howard was among the best, being named to the league's Best XI in 2001 and 2002. He became the first MLS-trained player to make the leap to a big name European team, going straight from the MetroStars to Manchester United. Howard spent 13 years in the Premier League with Manchester United and Everton before returning to Colorado to close out his career.

Kasey Keller also went to Europe as a keeper, but he did it before MLS even began. Keller was among the first Americans to go overseas to play, moving to Millwall in England in 1992. He played 16 professional seasons among England, Spain, and Germany before moving back to play in MLS for the Seattle Sounders. He won the 2011 Goalkeeper of the Year award at the age of almost 42.

## THE KEEPER THAT GOT AWAY

Brad Friedel is arguably the best goalkeeper in United States history. He played parts of just two seasons in MLS, in 1996 and 1997, because he was trying to get to the United Kingdom. The UK had strict rules about letting soccer players come there to work. The country refused to approve Friedel, even though Newcastle, Southampton, and Sunderland all tried to sign him. Finally, in 1997, the UK allowed him to move to Liverpool, ending his time with the Columbus Crew. Friedel spent 18 years in the Premier League, playing for Liverpool, Blackburn Rovers, Aston Villa, and Tottenham Hotspur.

# ALL-TIME LEADERS

## GOALS

1. Chris **WONDOLOWSKI**
2. Landon **DONOVAN**
3. Jeff **CUNNINGHAM**
4. Jaime **MORENO**
5. Kei **KAMARA**

## ASSISTS

1. Landon **DONOVAN**
2. Steve **RALSTON**
3. Brad **DAVIS**
4. Carlos **VALDERRAMA**
5. Predrag "Preki" **RADOSAVLJEVIĆ**

## SHUTOUTS

1. Nick **RIMANDO**
2. Kevin **HARTMAN**
3. Joe **CANNON**
4. Jon **BUSCH**
5. Stefan **FREI**

## SAVES

1. Nick **RIMANDO**
2. Kevin **HARTMAN**
3. Joe **CANNON**
4. Jon **BUSCH**
5. Tony **MEOLA**

# CHAPTER 6

# HOW MLS WORKS

The winner of the MLS postseason tournament wins the
league's ultimate prize, the MLS Cup. ▶

**F**ans of other sports leagues in the United States will understand the basics of how the MLS season works. The teams play 34 regular-season games. The top seven teams in each conference make the playoffs, and a knockout tournament crowns the MLS Cup champion. However, this setup is different from that in much of the rest of the world.

Take England's Premier League as an example. In the Premier League, the teams play the regular season, and then the team with the best record at the end of the season is the champion. There are no playoffs at all. Additionally, in the Premier League, each of the 20 teams plays the other 19 teams twice, once at home and once away.

Since MLS is bigger, not every team plays every other team twice. Instead, the 26 teams in MLS are split into two conferences, the Western Conference and the Eastern Conference. Each team plays the other 12 teams in its conference twice, once at home and once away. They play ten of the 12 teams in the other conference once more. This adds up to a total of 34 games.

## PLAYOFFS OR NOT?

Which setup is better is a matter of debate. To some, a setup like the Premier League's seems fairer. No team gets an advantage because of an easier or harder schedule than any other team's. It also makes the regular season more meaningful.

# MLS TEAMS

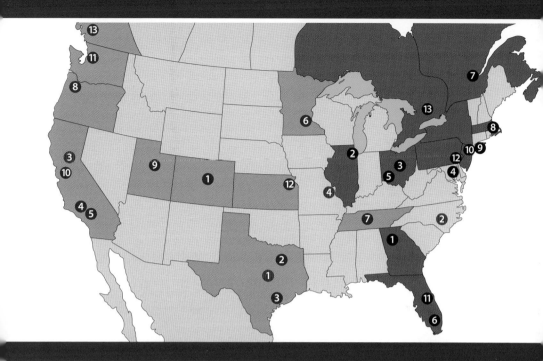

## WESTERN CONFERENCE

❶ Colorado Rapids
❷ FC Dallas
❸ Houston Dynamo
❹ LA Galaxy
❺ Los Angeles FC
❻ Minnesota United
❼ Nashville SC
❽ Portland Timbers
❾ Real Salt Lake
❿ San Jose Earthquakes
⓫ Seattle Sounders
⓬ Sporting Kansas City
⓭ Vancouver Whitecaps

## EASTERN CONFERENCE

❶ Atlanta United
❷ Chicago Fire FC
❸ Columbus Crew SC
❹ D.C. United
❺ FC Cincinnati
❻ Inter Miami CF
❼ Montreal Impact
❽ New England Revolution
❾ New York City FC
❿ New York Red Bulls
⓫ Orlando City
⓬ Philadelphia Union
⓭ Toronto FC

### FUTURE TEAMS

❶ Austin FC   ❷ Charlotte   ❸ Sacramento Republic FC   ❹ Saint Louis

On the flip side, quite often in the Premier League, one team has enough of a lead in the standings that the championship is awarded long before the end of the season. And since there's only one championship to play for, weaker teams tend to be eliminated from championship contention very early in the year.

Meanwhile, in a league like MLS, many teams stay in the chase for a playoff spot right up until the end of the season. Plus, the excitement of a postseason playoff tournament is undeniable. Everything is on the line, winner takes all. It's an excitement that the rest of the world knows well. Plenty of soccer's biggest competitions, including the World Cup and the UEFA Champions League, are decided by knockout tournaments.

## OTHER PRIZES ON THE LINE

The MLS Cup, while being the league's most prestigious prize, is not the only thing on the line each MLS season. Regular-season dominance is recognized too, in the form of the MLS Supporters' Shield. This is given to the team with the best record in the regular season. In a way, this trophy mimics the setup of leagues like the Premier League. Some people think that the Supporters' Shield should be more valuable than the MLS Cup, given that it rewards an entire season's worth of dominance, not just a few weeks' worth.

## A TROPHY INVENTED BY FANS

When MLS began in 1996, it handed out exactly one trophy: the MLS Cup. No recognition was given to the regular-season champions. In early 1997, fans from across North America began discussing, via email, creating a trophy that would honor the league's regular-season champion. Out of those discussions, the idea of the Supporters' Shield was born.

The fans raised money themselves to make the trophy. This included big donations from ESPN broadcaster Phil Schoen and MLS Commissioner Doug Logan. It was finally completed in early 1999, just in time to present it to the Los Angeles Galaxy, the 1998 winners of the trophy. Though neither the 1996 nor the 1997 champs ever held the trophy, their names have been on it from the beginning. Thanks to those supporters and their email list, the Shield has become a prestigious trophy in its own right.

MLS teams also compete in other knockout tournaments. Teams based in the United States play in the US Open Cup, and the three Canadian teams play in the Canadian Championship. The US Open Cup dates to 1913, when it was called the National Challenge Cup.

The US Open Cup and Canadian Championship are different because any team in those countries is eligible to enter, not just teams from MLS. This means that MLS teams are often matched up with teams from the United Soccer League (USL), which is the second division and third division league in the United States. They can also play teams from even lower leagues than that. Sometimes they even play amateur teams from local leagues around the country.

# CROSSING BORDERS

In addition to MLS and the domestic cup competitions, MLS teams play in international competitions. The main international competition is organized by the Confederation of North, Central American and Caribbean Association Football (Concacaf). This is the organization that runs soccer in the region. It organizes a tournament called the Concacaf Champions League (CCL), which includes the best club teams from all of the leagues in the region.

As of 2020, four teams from the United States and one team from Canada qualify for the CCL. The winner of the Canadian Championship qualifies from Canada. In the United States, the winner of the MLS Cup, the winner of the MLS Supporters' Shield, the winner of the US Open Cup, and the winner of the Eastern or Western

The UANL Tigres, a professional Mexican team, *in blue*, played against the Houston Dynamo in the 2019 Concacaf Champions League.

Conference (that didn't win the Supporters' Shield) qualifies for the tournament. If any team wins multiple trophies, or if a Canadian team wins them, the spot goes to the next-best US team in the MLS standings.

The best four teams from Liga MX, the Mexican soccer league, also qualify for the tournament, as well as seven other teams from Central America and the Caribbean. The 16 teams play a knockout tournament. Each game is a two-match series in which both teams get a home game,

MLS has always hoped that one of its teams could win the Concacaf Champions League. This would prove that MLS's teams could compete with the best from Mexico. Unfortunately, as of 2019, all 11 winners of the CCL have been from Liga MX. Prior to Concacaf introducing the Champions League format, it organized a tournament called the Champions Cup. Two MLS teams did win that trophy. D.C. United took it in 1998, and the Los Angeles Galaxy won in 2000.

and the team with the most total goals over the two matches wins.

# MLS AND LIGA MX, WORKING TOGETHER

MLS and Liga MX have often looked for ways to schedule more matches between teams in their respective leagues, beyond the Concacaf Champions League. Both leagues believe that teams in other parts of the world benefit hugely from having interleague competitions to bring more attention to their teams. Mexico, the United States, and Canada have tried to find ways to work together to do the same in North America.

The Liga MX champion and the MLS champion play a one-off match called the Campeones Cup. Mexico's season is split into two halves, so Mexico's entry in this match is determined by a game called the Campeón de Campeones, or "Champion of Champions." This matches the winners of each half of the season against each other. MLS's entrant is determined by the previous season's MLS Cup winner.

The two leagues also organized another competition, beginning in 2019, called the Leagues Cup. As of 2020, this will be a 16-team tournament. The eight best teams from MLS that don't qualify for the CCL will play in the Leagues Cup, along with the eight best teams from Mexico.

All that means that every MLS team could set out to win as many as five trophies in a single season. One team could win the MLS Cup, the Supporters' Shield, the US Open Cup or the Canadian Championship, the Concacaf Champions League or the Leagues Cup, and the Campeones Cup. For most teams, though, the MLS Cup is the main goal.

## TRIPLE TROPHIES

Only one MLS team has ever won three trophies in a single season: Toronto FC in 2017. The Reds lifted the MLS Cup, the Supporters' Shield, and the Canadian Championship that season. Eight other teams had managed two of the three, but Toronto was the first to get all three.[2] Toronto very nearly managed to continue its streak with two more the following year. The team lost the 2018 Concacaf Champions League finals to Chivas of Mexico, on penalties. They also lost the 2018 Campeones Cup to Tigres UANL.

# CHAPTER

# RIVALRIES AND CONTROVERSIES

Big rivalries have energized fan bases across MLS. ▶

What makes for a good sports rivalry? History helps, but it's not enough on its own. Championships are good, but it's rare to have a sports rivalry in which both teams are consistently competing for the title. The one thing that always causes rivalry, no matter the quality or the history of the teams, is geographical proximity. There's always plenty at stake because the fans know that they will have coworkers, friends, and even family on the other side of the rivalry. The same is true in MLS, where the three best rivalries in the league are between near neighbors.

## LOS ANGELES FC AND THE LOS ANGELES GALAXY

One major rivalry is between the Los Angeles Galaxy and Los Angeles FC. The El Tráfico games between them offer a contrast in styles. The Galaxy are the MLS originals, the team that's constantly benefited from an influx of star players. When the Galaxy wanted Landon Donovan, MLS found a way to maneuver him to Los Angeles. When the Galaxy wooed David Beckham, MLS introduced the Designated Player rule to allow the Galaxy to sign him to a huge contract. When the Galaxy wanted more star players, the league came up with another rule to allow LA to add more stars.

In many ways, LAFC are the opposite of the Galaxy. LAFC wear black at home, the Galaxy wear white. LAFC play near

LAFC fans sometimes point out that the Galaxy play their games in Carson, miles away from Los Angeles proper.

downtown, the Galaxy play in the suburbs. The Galaxy have championships, LAFC have very little history. And because of these differences, along with some great games between the two teams in their short history, the fans are passionate rivals. It's exactly the rivalry that MLS hoped to create when it put two teams in Los Angeles.

## NEW YORK CITY FC AND THE NEW YORK RED BULLS

On the other coast, MLS has done much the same as it did in Los Angeles. There's an MLS original team in the suburbs and an upstart team in the city. The New York Red Bulls are the renamed, rebranded New York/New Jersey MetroStars, one of the teams that founded MLS in 1996. Despite using the name New York, they have always played in New Jersey.

They used to play at Giants Stadium but are now at Red Bull Arena in Harrison, New Jersey.

New York City, meanwhile, play not just in New York but in Yankee Stadium, one of New York City's most unforgettable landmarks. They're the upstarts in this rivalry, having joined the league only in 2015. It didn't take long before things got heated. That summer, New York City FC (NYCFC) fans brawled with Red Bulls fans outside a restaurant in Newark, New Jersey, before a game. Red Bulls fans are disdainful of their upstart rivals. NYCFC fans love to point out that New York doesn't play in the town, or even the state, that the team is named for.

New York won five of the first six meetings between the teams. The games became known as the Hudson River Derby, named for the body of water that separates New York and New Jersey. These included a shocking 7–0 drubbing of NYCFC in Yankee Stadium. Red Bulls striker Bradley

## NAMING THE RIVALRY

It's not just El Tráfico and the Hudson River Derby that have catchy names. Some other rivalry games include the Atlantic Cup, for the New York Red Bulls and D.C. United; the Texas Derby, for Houston and Dallas; the California Clásico, for San Jose and the Los Angeles Galaxy; and the Rocky Mountain Cup, for Real Salt Lake and Colorado. The newest rivalry in MLS is the game between expansion Cincinnati and Columbus. Its name comes from a phrase on a religious billboard that stands next to Interstate 71 between the cities: Hell is Real.

Wright-Phillips scored twice in that game, which seems appropriate since the player known as BWP has saved his best for games between the two teams. As of 2019, Wright-Phillips had scored 11 times in 11 games against New York's across-the-river rivals.

## SEATTLE, PORTLAND, AND THE BEST MLS HAS TO OFFER

In contrast to the New York and Los Angeles rivalries, the Portland Timbers and the Seattle Sounders aren't crosstown rivals. It's a three-hour drive from one city to the other. The two cities have a long-standing rivalry, though, even outside of soccer. When it comes to Sounders–Timbers games, this is the rare MLS rivalry that dates back even farther than the league, all the way to 1975.

Back then, both teams were in the NASL. It was the Timbers' first year in the league. By the teams' third meeting, Seattle coach John Best was already declaring, "Seattle playing Portland has become as heated as any neighborhood-division rivalry they have in England. It's Liverpool playing Everton."[1] *Sports Illustrated* writer Pat Putnam, writing about Seattle's 3–2 overtime win, wrote that "fights began breaking out all over."[2] It was a preview of many conflicts to come.

That Seattle-Portland rivalry continued through the NASL and through the short-lived leagues that followed it.

The Timbers taunted their rivals in Seattle with a billboard in 2011.

It carried over into the second division from 2001–2008. It finally made its way into MLS, as Seattle joined the league in 2009 and Portland joined in 2011. That was the year that Timbers fans paid for a billboard near Seattle's stadium that said, "PORTLAND, OREGON—SOCCER CITY USA 2011."[3]

Until Atlanta entered the league, Seattle had far and away the biggest crowds in MLS. Portland couldn't match those numbers, but the team made up for it with the atmosphere at Providence Park. Put it all together with more than four decades of rivalry games, and it's enough to make this the best rivalry in American soccer.

## CONTROVERSIAL MOMENTS

Given that MLS is organized as a single entity in which the league owns all the clubs, it often has the ability to make decisions about where a player should play. This power

## CONFLICT IN THE PACIFIC NORTHWEST

It's hard to pick out the best moment in the Sounders–Timbers rivalry. One of the best came in 2009, in a US Open Cup game in Portland. Just 48 seconds in, Seattle's Roger Levesque scored right in front of Portland's diehards. Then he celebrated the goal by imitating a falling tree as teammate Nate Jaqua pretended to chop him down.

Two years later, when Portland visited Seattle after joining MLS, the Sounders fans unveiled a huge banner proclaiming their "decades of dominance" over Portland. The display included a special banner of Levesque's face, with the words "48 Seconds."[4] So despised was Levesque in Portland that in 2007, when he played a game for the Timbers as a "guest player" for the lower-division side, the Portland fans booed him every single time he touched the ball.

was reduced with later rule changes, but there's still bound to be controversy as players are moved from one team to another. The best example of this might have happened in 1999 when Carlos Valderrama moved from Tampa Bay to Miami. Valderrama was feuding with coach Ivo Wortmann, and everyone knew it. Miami couldn't find a team to trade him to. League commissioner Doug Logan stepped in and simply reassigned Valderrama back to Tampa Bay.

A similar controversy happened in 2014, when US men's national team standout Jermaine Jones wanted to come to MLS. Jones met with the Chicago Fire and negotiated a contract with the league. But the New England Revolution also wanted Jones, who was willing to go either place. With no hard-and-fast rule about where to place Jones, and two teams wanting his services, the league made up a rule on the spot. It conducted a blind draw to determine which team got him. In the end, Jones went to New England.

MLS's strange rule changes have also caused controversy. One example is the short-lived rule that allowed a fourth substitution as long as the fourth substitution was a goalkeeper. In 2003, then MetroStars head coach Bob Bradley took advantage of the rule in a novel way. In an overtime game against D.C. United, Bradley had goalkeeper Tim Howard switch positions with midfielder Mark Lisi. He then substituted striker Eddie Gaven in for Lisi. Gaven put on the goalkeeper jersey and gloves—for all of ten seconds. The MetroStars immediately kicked the ball out so that Howard could switch back to goalkeeper and Gaven could play the field. He ended up scoring the winning overtime goal. It earned Bradley the nickname "Cheatin' Bob" from the D.C. United fans.[5] It also led MLS to eliminate the rule.

## WHAT'S IN A NAME?

When the San Jose Earthquakes moved to Houston for the 2006 season, the new team announced that they would be called Houston 1836. This was a reference to the year the city was founded. However, the name caused an uproar among Mexican Americans in the community. They were quick to point out that 1836 was also a reference to a number of anti-Mexican events, like Texas independence and the Battle of the Alamo. Facing pressure, Houston changed their name to the Houston Dynamo.

# RICARDO CLARK LOSES IT

Perhaps the wildest moment in league history was also one of the most understandable. At least, it made sense to anyone who'd played against Carlos Ruiz. The Guatemalan striker was a world-class pest. He was the type who'd elbow a player in the ribs when the ref wasn't looking, or kick an opponent in the ankle at an opportune moment and then roll around as if he'd been shot if the opponent dared retaliate. When Ruiz was playing for Dallas in 2007, Houston Dynamo midfielder Ricardo Clark had finally had enough.

Late in the game, Ruiz piled into Clark on a free kick, kneeing him in the back and knocking him to the ground. Clark, as so many defenders before had dreamed of doing, lost it. He sprang off the ground and booted Ruiz as hard as he could in the shoulder. Ruiz, for his part, acted as if he'd been kicked directly in the face. Clark was suspended for nine games and missed Houston's run to the MLS Cup that season. He and Ruiz made up a few years later.

## THE LONGEST SUSPENSION IN MLS HISTORY

Only one suspension in MLS history has been longer than Ricardo Clark's nine games. In 2011, defender Brian Mullan delivered a vicious tackle on Seattle attacker Steve Zaukuani, breaking Zaukuani's leg. Mullan was suspended for ten games. Zaukuani, who was in only his third year as a pro, was out for 18 months while recovering. He was never the same when he came back. He retired in 2014.

# CHAPTER 8

## HOW THEY GOT HERE

The MLS SuperDraft is one of several ways that new players join MLS. ▶

In other American pro sports, there are standard paths that players take to get to the big leagues. In football or basketball it involves getting a college scholarship and becoming a college athlete. Baseball players prove themselves in the minor leagues. Hockey players play through a combination of juniors, college, and the minors.

In soccer in the United States and Canada, the standard path of going first to college, then to pro soccer still exists. But there are many other ways into the league. The yearly draft for college players sometimes seems like an afterthought, whereas in other sports the draft is a major event.

## THE HISTORY OF THE SUPERDRAFT

In the first four years of MLS, the league had two drafts. There was one for college players and one for players who had already graduated and might be playing in other leagues. It wasn't until they combined the two, merging the College Draft and the Supplemental Draft in 2000, that they created the SuperDraft, which included all players.

The league also held an Inaugural Player Draft in its first year. The first pick in that draft, US national team legend Brian McBride, turned out to be a pretty good one. But for the most part, the history of Number 1 draft picks has been uneven. Some, such as Marvell Wynne and Maurice Edu, turned out to be standout pros. Others, including Steve Shak and Nikolas Besagno, never made much of an impact. With the rise of academies and of signing young players from overseas, the SuperDraft seems to decrease in importance every year.

Each January, MLS holds a draft for college players called the MLS SuperDraft. College players who have graduated, as well as select underclassmen, are eligible for the draft. As of 2020, there were four rounds in the draft. However, teams have placed less and less of an emphasis on acquiring players through the draft. It has become common for teams to not even use their picks in later rounds. In 2020, there were 104 draft slots, but only 77 players selected. Only ten of a possible 26 picks were made in the fourth round.[1]

## YOUNG PLAYERS

Often young players don't need to head to college at all before they turn pro. In some cases, they barely need to go to high school. In August 2017, Gianluca Busio signed a contract with Sporting Kansas City (SKC) at the age of 15. This made him the second-youngest player in MLS history to sign with a pro club. He wasn't just speculation for the future, either. He made an impact within just a few years. In 2019, at the age of just 17, he played in 22 games for SKC, scoring three goals.[2]

The youngest player ever to sign with MLS was once perhaps the most famous MLS player of all. His name was Freddy Adu, and he was the Number 1 pick in the 2004 MLS SuperDraft. He was also just 14 years old. Amazingly, he played in 30 games for D.C. United that year. He became the

Adu showed great potential, but many people felt he didn't live up to the hype in MLS.

league's youngest-ever goal scorer when he scored his first goal two months before his fifteenth birthday.

The hype was overwhelming. Adu appeared in national advertisements for Pepsi and Nike. He was getting paid far more than his more experienced teammates. He played three seasons in D.C., then part of one season for Real Salt Lake, and then he was off to Europe and Benfica, one of Portugal's biggest clubs. From then on, it was a journey downward to lesser and lesser European teams. Everywhere, Adu was dogged by a reputation for not wanting to work hard, for only wanting to score goals, and for standing around when he didn't have the ball.

Adu returned to MLS in 2011, scoring seven times over two seasons with Philadelphia, but he never lived up to the promise he had shown as a 14-year-old. So many people thought that Adu would be the first truly great American soccer player, but it hasn't worked out that way. Still, MLS teams have continued to sign young players in the modern era. In 2019, two 14-year-olds signed MLS contracts.

## ACADEMIES AND HOMEGROWN PLAYERS

In 2008, MLS introduced a new rule called the Homegrown Player rule. This allowed teams to sign players without them having to go through the draft as long as the player had trained with the team's academy for at least one year. The intent of this rule was to give teams an incentive to develop youth players via their academies. This is a common system throughout the soccer world, where clubs run youth teams to try to identify talent and then bring those players up to

# CLINT
# DEMPSEY

Some American soccer stars leave for Europe and never return. Some find they can't hack it overseas and have to come back. But Clint Dempsey developed in America, moved on to bigger things in Europe, and then came home again to be a star.

Dempsey, from Nacogdoches, Texas, grew up making a six-hour round trip to Dallas for club soccer practices. His development came as much from playing Sunday league games against grown men as it did from club soccer. After becoming a small-college star, he took MLS by storm. He then moved to England for six years and became a standout player there.

He could have found another club in England and then only come back to MLS when no one wanted him. Instead, he chose to return to MLS and play for Seattle, where he starred for five more years. In many ways, he's the example of what MLS hopes for in its players. They are able to develop at home and can make it overseas, but they also want to play in MLS.

Dempsey raised a Sounders scarf before a 2013 game in a ceremony celebrating his decision to join the team.

the first team. Rather than leave development to youth teams and college teams, the Homegrown rule would allow teams to develop their own players.

Gianluca Busio was just such a player. Other MLS standouts, such as Jordan Morris with the Seattle Sounders, were also signed in this way. It has been lucrative for clubs like the Vancouver Whitecaps. After developing winger Alphonso Davies at the club, they sold him to German team Bayern Munich for an MLS-record transfer fee.

## THE MODEL ACADEMY

In 2013, the Philadelphia Union took a novel step. Not only would they open their own academy program, they'd set up a private high school to go with it. Called YSC Academy, it makes it easier for Union youth players to combine school and soccer. Some of Philadelphia's bright young stars, such as Auston Trusty and Mark McKenzie, have been products of the school. Other MLS teams have set up their own, similar schools.

# EUROPE, LATIN AMERICA, AND THE WORLD

MLS has always been able to attract veteran players from Europe and Latin America. When fans think about overseas players, those are the players they tend to think of—names such as David Beckham, Carlos Valderrama, Robbie Keane, Marco Etcheverry, and Rafa Marquez. However, it's not just big names at the end of their careers who are coming to

MLS. In recent years, MLS has attracted younger players who are looking to make a mark in the league.

A contrast between two Italians that made their mark on MLS demonstrates this shift. Roberto Donadoni was the biggest European star to join MLS in 1996, its first year, but by that time he was already 32. The former AC Milan and Italy midfielder, whom French great Michel Platini once called "the best Italian footballer of the 1990s," played well for the MetroStars.[3] He made the league's Best XI in his first year. But he lasted just two seasons before retiring and turning to coaching.

Sebastian Giovinco, meanwhile, arrived in Toronto from Italian powerhouse Juventus in 2015, having just turned 28. He was still in his prime, and it showed. Giovinco, nicknamed "Atomic Ant" for his small stature, started dominating the league. In four seasons with Toronto, he scored double-digit goals every season, dished out

## THEY COME FROM ALL OVER

In 2019, there were players from more than 70 different countries playing in MLS. Just over half come from North America, with three-quarters of those players hailing from the United States. Besides the United States and Canada, the country with the most players was Argentina, with 33. The US state that gave the league the most players was California, with 62. No other state or Canadian province provided more than 25.

double-digit assists in all but one season, won the 2015 MVP award, and made the league's Best XI three times.

Since entering the league in 2017, Atlanta United has been at the forefront of bringing young South American players to MLS. These players not only are current standouts but also represent an investment for the future. Within three years, the team signed players such as Miguel Almirón (23 years old when he signed), Ezequiel Barco (18), Josef Martínez (24), and Pity Martínez (25). All of them were stars in South America. Pity Martínez was even the reigning South American Player of the Year when he signed. As MLS looks into the future, the changing face of what it means to be an MLS player—and what it means to be an MLS team—will drive the league forward.

## PLAYER SALARIES

The minimum salary in MLS in 2019 was $56,250. This was mostly for reserve players who occupy spots 21 through 30 on the team roster. The top salary in the league was for Zlatan Ibrahimović, who was guaranteed $7.2 million for 2019. Designated Players tend to make the most, but salaries have been growing for other players too. Between 2014 and 2019, the average salary for a senior player who was not a Designated Player jumped from $138,140 to $345,867.[4]

# WHAT'S NEXT?

Fans welcomed several new teams, including
FC Cincinnati, to MLS in the late 2010s and early 2020s. ▶

**M**LS has changed enormously over its history. It began as a struggling attempt to overcome the failures of the past. It tentatively developed into a stable league. By 2019, it was growing explosively. The league has moved from football stadiums to suburban soccer stadiums to downtown soccer stadiums. The players are no longer just American college kids with a sprinkling of South American and European veterans. Now there's a mix of young players from different backgrounds and at every stage of development.

## ATLANTA UNITED: A VISION OF THE FUTURE

Atlanta United FC, one of the league's newest clubs, may provide a vision of what the future will hold. Despite being a recent expansion team, Atlanta did not endure the traditional growing pains of an expansion franchise. They made the playoffs in their first year. They won the MLS Cup in their second, just barely missing out on the Supporters' Shield. In their third, they won the US Open Cup and

### THE BIGGEST LEAGUE IN THE WORLD

Until the 2019–20 season, the Argentina Primera Liga had 30 teams. The newly named Superliga Argentina, however, has just 24. This means that when MLS adds its twenty-fifth and twenty-sixth teams in 2020, it will have more teams than any other top division league in the world.

the Campeón de Campeones. It's a trophy haul that makes even long-established MLS teams envious.

Atlanta made a decision to do things a little differently when they came into the league. Usually, expansion teams would sign one or two big names to help sell tickets, surround them with also-ran players, and hope to be good enough to not be terrible. Take Orlando City, who signed Brazilian star Kaka for the 2015 season. New York City FC, which signed big name European veterans David Villa and Frank Lampard, did the same.

Atlanta instead hired the best coach they could, Gerardo "Tata" Martino, who'd coached FC Barcelona in Spain as well as the Argentina national team. Leaning on his reputation, Atlanta paid big to acquire young South American stars like Josef Martínez and Miguel Almirón. Atlanta convinced them

## THE STRANGE NICKNAMES OF MLS

Most of MLS's franchises have either traditional sports nicknames (such as the Seattle Sounders or Portland Timbers) or traditional English-style soccer nicknames (such as Orlando City and the three Uniteds—D.C., Minnesota, and Atlanta). A few teams have branched out to try to borrow soccer nicknames from elsewhere in the world. The first word of Real Salt Lake is given a Spanish pronunciation, like Real Madrid or Real Sociedad in Spain. Sporting Kansas City is a play on team names like Portugal's Sporting Lisbon. Inter Miami CF, whose full name is Club Internacional de Fútbol Miami, is an allusion both to Italian giants Inter Milan and Brazilian heavyweights Internacional.

that they could star in MLS under Martino and then move on to bigger teams.

Almirón serves as a perfect example of why Atlanta might do this. Atlanta paid an $8 million transfer fee for the Paraguayan star in 2016.[1] Almirón made the league's Best XI in both 2017 and 2018, helping lead the Five Stripes to the MLS Cup in 2018. Then, prior to the 2019 season, Atlanta sold him to Newcastle United in the Premier League for an MLS-record $27 million.[2] By 2019, Martínez was still in Atlanta, where he made the Best XI three seasons in a row, scored an astonishing 77 goals in 83 games, and won the 2018 league MVP award.

## A GROWING LEAGUE, A GROWING SPORT

The league's rapid expansion is set to continue. It added New York City FC and Orlando City SC in 2015. Atlanta United and Minnesota United joined in 2017. Los Angeles FC came aboard in 2018, as did FC Cincinnati in 2019. In 2020, Inter Miami CF and Nashville SC were set to join the league. In 2021, Austin FC and Charlotte were planned to be added. In 2022, franchises in Saint Louis and Sacramento were slated to join the league.

New stadiums will continue to go up. Most will be built by expansion teams, but some older teams will do the same. In 2019, Columbus were already working on a replacement

# THE FUTURE OF THE LEAGUE'S SCHEDULE

With more and more teams coming into the league, MLS did not have a balanced schedule in 2020. Teams played the teams in their conference twice, but they were not able to play all of the teams in the other conference even once.

One solution that many soccer fans are familiar with involves dividing the league into multiple divisions. In this scenario, the best teams from the lower division are promoted to the higher one, while the worst teams from the higher division are relegated to the lower one. This system of promotion and relegation is in use in almost every other country that plays soccer. However, none of the other countries have a system like MLS, where the league centrally owns all the teams.

MLS commissioner Don Garber has been firm in saying that promotion and relegation doesn't make sense. The financial realities of the league back him up. But that hasn't stopped many fans from hoping that MLS might someday look more like other leagues around the world.

for the first MLS stadium ever built. Chicago was moving out of the stadium they built in the suburbs. New England was heavily rumored to be ready to finally move out of their NFL-stadium home, too.

Soccer's popularity will continue to grow in the United States. A Gallup poll in early 2018 found that 7 percent of adult Americans said soccer was their favorite sport to watch. This put the sport behind football, basketball, and baseball. However, among those under the age of 55, soccer was more popular than baseball and virtually tied with basketball.[3] The challenge for MLS will be to get people to watch its games rather than soccer games from other leagues around the world.

## THE FUTURE OF MLS

What's next for Major League Soccer might be more of the same. More growth, in terms of both fan interest and the sheer number of franchises, is likely. More stars from overseas, as well as new ones developing from the United States and Canada, will enter the league. More people will watch the league's games, including both fans of other leagues and fans of other American sports.

The league has learned the lessons of the leagues that came before it. It's avoided pitfalls and taken advantage of increased fan interest in soccer. The United States and Canada still aren't soccer-crazy nations compared with traditional strongholds like England, Germany, and Argentina. But after nearly a quarter century in business,

**SOCCER ON TV**

TV ratings for MLS games usually trail the TV ratings for Liga MX and the Premier League. While this doesn't take into account local broadcasts in each city, it's safe to say that many Americans are watching games from Mexico and England each week. Some of these fans are MLS fans too, perhaps even fans who are attending MLS games. But one of the key future challenges for MLS is to get fans watching the league on TV too.

As MLS moved into the 2020s, American professional soccer had more fans, was earning more money, and was a bigger cultural force than ever before.

MLS has boosted the number of American and Canadian soccer fans higher than ever.

## MLS AND COVID-19

In early 2020, a new disease called COVID-19 swept the globe, leaving millions of people infected and hundreds of thousands dead. To slow its spread, health officials instructed people to maintain physical distance between each other. This had a dramatic impact on the sports world, including MLS. On March 12, the league announced that its two-week-old season would be suspended for 30 days. One week later, it extended the suspension to May 10. But in mid-April, a league statement cast doubt even on this plan: "Although we hoped to return to play in mid-May, that is extremely unlikely based on the guidance of federal and local public health authorities."[4] COVID-19 paralyzed the MLS and sports leagues worldwide.

# ESSENTIAL FACTS

## Significant Events

o The United States hosted the 1994 FIFA World Cup, and as part of its bid for hosting, it promised to start a new professional soccer league. There had been pro soccer leagues in the United States and Canada before, some of which were very popular for a short time, but all of the previous attempts at a league had failed.

o Major League Soccer kicked off in 1996 with ten teams and added two more in 1998.

o After the 2001 season, the league folded teams in Miami and Tampa Bay due to early struggles.

o In 2002, the USA reached the quarterfinals of the World Cup, and stars from that team, such as Landon Donovan, gave MLS fans new players to follow.

o Superstar David Beckham joined the Los Angeles Galaxy in 2007, giving the league more media coverage and attention than it had ever seen before.

o Toronto FC joined MLS in 2007, and the Seattle Sounders joined the league in 2009. Together they helped pave the way for a new kind of MLS club.

## Key Players

o The MLS most valuable player (MVP) award is now named for Landon Donovan. He retired as the league's all-time leader in both goals (145) and assists (136).

o Carlos Valderrama was the league's best-known Latin American star when MLS kicked off in 1996. Valderrama captained the Colombian national team in three World Cups and played for seven seasons in MLS, winning the 1996 MVP award.

o Tim Howard got his start with the MetroStars in New York, making the league's Best XI in 2001 and 2002 before moving to Manchester United in England and becoming the first MLS-trained player to play for a top European team.

- Predrag "Preki" Radosavljević won the league MVP award twice, in 1997 and 2003. He was already 33 years old and an indoor-soccer star by the time MLS kicked off in 1996, and he was the league's top scorer in 2003 at the age of 40.

- As of the end of the 2019 season, Carlos Vela had scored 48 goals for Los Angeles FC in just 59 games over two seasons. He was named the league's MVP in 2019 for scoring 34 times to lead the league.

## Key Teams

- D.C. United dominated the early years of MLS, winning the MLS Cup in 1996, 1997, and 1999. United also won the Supporters' Shield in 1997 and 1999, as well as the US Open Cup in 1996. It later won the US Open Cup again in 2008 and 2013.

- With players like Landon Donovan and David Beckham, the Los Angeles Galaxy have often been the most star-studded team in MLS. They have won the MLS Cup five times, the most of any team, and have also won four Supporters' Shields and two US Open Cups.

- As of 2019, the Seattle Sounders have never missed the playoffs in 11 years as an MLS team. During that span, the Sounders have won two MLS Cups, a Supporters' Shield, and four US Open Cups.

- In 2017, Toronto FC became the first MLS team to win three trophies in a single year, taking home the MLS Cup, the Supporters' Shield, and the Canadian Championship.

## Quote

"English football is a gray game played on a gray day before gray people. American soccer is a colorful game played on a sunny day before colorful people."

—*Rodney Marsh, English soccer player and NASL star*

# GLOSSARY

## amateur
Related to competing in a sport without payment.

## assist
A pass from one teammate to another that directly leads to a goal.

## Best XI
An all-star team for a soccer league. The best players at each position are named to the Best XI, pronounced "Best Eleven," team at the end of the season.

## debut
A person's first appearance in a specific role.

## diehard
An extremely dedicated fan.

## expansion
The addition of a new team to a league.

## first division
The soccer leagues in most countries are organized into different divisions, with the biggest, most important teams in the top division, or first division. In the United States and Canada, the current first division is Major League Soccer.

## knockout
The stage of a competition in which one loss eliminates a team.

## midfielder
A player who plays mostly in the middle third of the field. This player is responsible for linking the defenders with the forwards, who try to score.

## penalty area
An area marked with lines on the field, 18 yards from each side of the goal and 18 yards from the front. Any foul in the penalty area results in a penalty kick for the team that is fouled.

## points

In soccer, teams usually get three points in the standings for a win, one point for a tie, and no points for losses. The team that wins the league is the team with the most points.

## recession

A period of negative economic growth and, usually, low demand for goods and high unemployment.

## sanctioning

Making the rules and the structure for a sport.

## stoppage time

Also known as added time, a number of minutes tacked on to the end of a half for stoppages that occurred during play from injuries, free kicks, and goals.

## striker

A player whose primary responsibility is to create scoring chances and score goals.

## transfer fee

The money that one team will pay another team to trade, or transfer, a player.

## turnover

When one team gives the ball away to the other team accidentally.

## winger

A player who plays mostly along the edges, or wings, of the field. This player is often charged with going around the side of the defense or crossing the ball to the front of the goal from the edge of the field.

# ADDITIONAL RESOURCES

## Selected Bibliography

Dure, Beau. *Long-Range Goals: The Success Story of Major League Soccer.* Potomac Books, 2010.

Pentz, Matt. *The Sound and the Glory.* ECW Press, 2019.

Plenderleith, Ian. *Rock N Roll Soccer: The Short Life and Fast Times of the North American Soccer League.* St. Martin's Press, 2015.

## Further Readings

Killion, Ann. *Champions of Men's Soccer.* Philomel Books, 2018.

Latham, Andrew. *Soccer Smarts for Kids.* Rockridge Press, 2016.

Lloyd, Carli. *All Heart: My Dedication and Determination to Become One of Soccer's Best.* HMH Books for Young Readers, 2016.

## Online Resources

To learn more about MLS, please visit **abdobooklinks.com** or scan this QR code. These links are routinely monitored and updated to provide the most current information available.

## More Information

For more information on this subject, contact or visit the following organizations:

### Hap Meyer Soccer Collection
Lovejoy Library, Southern Illinois University Edwardsville
30 Hairpin Dr.
Edwardsville, IL 62026
618-650-4636
digitallis.isg.siue.edu/items/show/2266

The Hap Meyer Soccer Collection contains artifacts related to the early days of soccer in the United States.

### National Soccer Hall of Fame
9200 World Cup Way, Suite 600
Frisco, TX 75033
469-365-0043
nationalsoccerhof.com

The National Soccer Hall of Fame honors the best soccer players in American history as well as the people who built the game of soccer in the United States.

# SOURCE NOTES

## CHAPTER 1. EL TRÁFICO 2018

1. Adam Serrano. "Zlatan Ibrahimović Takes Out Full-Page Ad in Los Angeles Times: 'Los Angeles, You're Welcome.'" *MLS*, 23 Mar. 2018, lagalaxy.com. Accessed 27 Jan. 2020.

2. Jon Marthaler. "Meet Zlatan Ibrahimovic, The L.A. Galaxy's New Braggadocious Striker Who Backs Up His Big Talk with Bigger Play." *Star Tribune*, 10 Apr. 2018, startribune.com. Accessed 27 Jan. 2020.

3. Jonathan Tannenwald. "Watch: Zlatan Ibrahimovic Goals Lead LA Galaxy over LAFC, 4–3." *Philadelphia Inquirer*, 31 Mar. 2018, inquirer.com. Accessed 27 Jan. 2020.

4. "Olympic Football Tournament Los Angeles 1984." *FIFA*, 2015, fifa.com. Accessed 27 Jan. 2020.

## CHAPTER 2. AMERICAN PROFESSIONAL SOCCER

1. David Wangerin. *Soccer in a Football World: The Story of America's Forgotten Game*. Temple University Press, 2008. 59.

2. Michael Lewis. "William Cox: The Eccentric Architect of Professional US Soccer." *Guardian*, 26 July 2016, theguardian.com. Accessed 27 Jan. 2020.

3. Ian Plenderleith. *Rock 'n' Roll Soccer: The Short Life and Fast Times of the North American Soccer League*. St. Martin's Press, 2015. 126.

4. Plenderleith, *Rock 'n' Roll Soccer,* 321.

5. "Attendance Project: NASL." *Kenn*, 2020, kenn.com. Accessed 27 Jan. 2020.

6. Plenderleith, *Rock 'n' Roll Soccer,* 289.

## CHAPTER 3. NEW LEAGUE, NEW RULES, NEW TEAMS

1. Ian Plenderleith. *Rock 'n' Roll Soccer: The Short Life and Fast Times of the North American Soccer League*. St. Martin's Press, 2015. 212.

2. Beau Dure. *Long-Range Goals: The Success Story of Major League Soccer*. Potomac Books, 2010. 12.

3. Dure, *Long-Range Goals*, 46.

4. Grant Wahl. *The Beckham Experiment: How the World's Most Famous Athlete Tried to Conquer America*. Crown Books, 2009. 2.

5. Wahl, *The Beckham Experiment*, 8.

6. Graham Ruthven. "Why Many LA Galaxy Fans Don't Believe David Beckham Deserves a Statue." *Guardian*, 4 Mar. 2019, theguardian.com. Accessed 27 Jan. 2020.

7. "MLS Announces Plans to Expand to 30 Teams." *MLS*, 18 Apr. 2019, mlssoccer.com. Accessed 19 Feb. 2020.

## CHAPTER 4. CATHEDRALS OF AMERICAN SOCCER

1. "2019 MLS Attendance." *Soccer Stadium Digest*, 2020, soccerstadiumdigest.com. Accessed 27 Jan. 2020.

2. Beau Dure. *Long-Range Goals: The Success Story of Major League Soccer.* Potomac Books, 2010. 69.

3. "Seattle Sounders Are 29th-Most Attended Club in World." *MLS*, 16 Apr. 2019, soundersfc.com. Accessed 27 Jan. 2020.

4. Doug Roberson. "Atlanta United's Attendance 10th Higest Among World's Clubs." *Atlanta Journal-Constitution*, 16 Apr. 2019, ajc.com. Accessed 27 Jan. 2020.

## CHAPTER 5. GREATS OF THE GAME

1. "All-Time." *MLS*, 2020, mlssoccer.com. Accessed 27 Jan. 2020.

2. Scott French. "LA Glaxay's Zlatan Ibrahimovic: 'I Think I'm the Best-Ever Player in MLS.'" *MLS*, 16 Sept. 2019, mlssoccer.com. Accessed 27 Jan. 2020.

3. "MLS 2019 Year-End Awards Finalists Revealed: Ibrahimovic, Vela, Martinez up for MVP." *MLS*, 14 Oct. 2019, mlssoccer.com. Accessed 27 Jan. 2020.

## CHAPTER 6. HOW MLS WORKS

1. "Rochester Rhinos Pay Tribute to 1999 U.S. Open Cup Team." *Democrat & Chronicle*, 29 June 2013, democratandchronicle.com. Accessed 27 Jan. 2020.

2. Alicia Rodriguez. "Toronto FC Win First Domestic Treble in MLS History." *MLS*, 9 Dec. 2017, mlssoccer.com. Accessed 27 Jan. 2020.

## CHAPTER 7. RIVALRIES AND CONTROVERSIES

1. Pat Putnam. "What A Battle in Seattle." *Sports Illustrated Vault*, 11 Aug. 1975, si.com. Accessed 27 Jan. 2020.

2. Putnam, "What A Battle in Seattle."

3. Grant Wahl. "A Pacific Passion Play." *Sports Illustrated Vault*, 23 May 2011, si.com. Accessed 27 Jan. 2020.

4. "Top 10 Roger Levesque Moments -#1." *YouTube*, uploaded by Seattle Sounders FC, 5 Oct. 2012, youtube.com. Accessed 27 Jan. 2020.

5. Craig Merz and Jonah Freedman. "Top Atlantic Cup Moments: 'Cheatin' Bob' Bradley and Eddie Gaven's Confusing 10 Seconds in Goal." *MLS*, 14 Mar. 2013, mlssoccer.com. Accessed 27 Jan. 2020.

## CHAPTER 8. HOW THEY GOT HERE

1. "2019 Superdraft." *MLS*, 2020, mlssoccer.com. Accessed 27 Jan. 2020.

2. "Gianluca Busio." *MLS*, 2020, sportingkc.com. Accessed 27 Jan. 2020.

3. Clemente Lisi. "The Understated Finesse of Roberto Donadoni." *These Football Times*, 3 Aug. 2018, thesefootballtimes.co. Accessed 27 Jan. 2020.

4. "Salary Guide." *MLSPA*, 13 Sept. 2019, mlsplayers.org. Accessed 27 Jan. 2020.

## CHAPTER 9. WHAT'S NEXT?

1. Jeff Carlisle. "Atlanta United Completes Signing of Paraguay Star Miguel Almiron." *ESPN*, 5 Dec. 2016, espn.co.uk. Accessed 27 Jan. 2020.

2. "Miguel Almiron: Newcastle United Sign Playmaker for Club Record Fee of £20M." *BBC*, 31 Jan. 2019, bbc.com. Accessed 27 Jan. 2020.

3. Jim Norman. "Football Still Americans' Favorite Sport to Watch." *Gallup*, 4 Jan. 2018, news.gallup.com. Accessed 27 Jan. 2020.

4. Tyler Conway. "MLS Calls Mid-May Return 'Extremely Unlikely' Because of COVID-19 Pandemic." *Bleacher Report*, 14 Apr. 2020, bleacherreport.com. Accessed 28 Apr. 2020.

# INDEX

# ABOUT THE AUTHOR

## Jon Marthaler

Jon Marthaler has been a freelance sportswriter for more than 15 years. He has written eight sports books for kids about MLS, world soccer, and many other sports, and he writes a weekly soccer column for the *Star Tribune* in Minneapolis, Minnesota. Jon lives in Saint Paul, Minnesota, with his wife and their two kids.